GAME ON!

Read more by Himanjali Sankar

For younger readers

The Stupendous Timetelling Superdog
Missing! A Magnificent Superdog

For young adults

Talking of Muskaan
The Lies We Tell

Scan QR code to access the
Penguin Random House India website

HIMANJALI SANKAR

Illustrations by Chetan Sharma

An imprint of Penguin Random House

DUCKBILL BOOKS

Duckbill Books is an imprint of the Penguin Random House group of companies whose addresses can be found at global.penguinrandomhouse.com

Published by Penguin Random House India Pvt. Ltd
4th Floor, Capital Tower 1, MG Road,
Gurugram 122 002, Haryana, India

First published in Duckbill Books by
Penguin Random House India 2025

Copyright © Himanjali Sankar 2025
Illustrations copyright © Chetan Sharma 2025

Himanjali Sankar asserts the moral right to be
identified as the author of this work.

All rights reserved

10 9 8 7 6 5 4 3 2 1

This is a work of fiction. Names, characters, places and incidents are either the product of the author's imagination or are used fictitiously and any resemblance to any actual person, living or dead, events or locales is entirely coincidental.

Please note that no part of this book may be used or reproduced in any manner for the purpose of training artificial intelligence technologies or systems.

ISBN 9780143476672

Typeset in Georgia Pro by DiTech Publishing Services Pvt. Ltd
Printed at Thomson Press India Ltd, New Delhi

This book is sold subject to the condition that it shall not, by way of trade or otherwise, be lent, resold, hired out, or otherwise circulated without the publisher's prior consent in any form of binding or cover other than that in which it is published and without a similar condition including this condition being imposed on the subsequent purchaser.

www.penguin.co.in

Before it Began

No one stirs. They hear him ask the question but neither Sammy nor Simmy get up.

'Can I have a glass of water?' Papa asks again, thinking the kids hadn't heard.

'You can,' replies Sammy and goes back to her phone.

'Yes, you really can,' adds Simmy, giggling, and goes back to his painting.

'Woof,' says Bobby. She would have got a glass of water for Papa if she had opposable thumbs, but she doesn't. Luckily, since her own bowl of water is always kept filled by Ma, she doesn't have to ask anyone for water or fetch it for herself. Bobby rules.

Ma frowns and looks at the kids. She has been jabbing at her office game console and muttering to herself.

'Another stressful day at EIGDC?' Papa asks.

Ma works at the Ethical-Immersive Game Development Centre, where she is in charge of the team that designs video games.

'You can say that again,' Ma says. 'Remember that humanoid robot we created?'

Sammy looks up. 'Yes! Your boss named him Dinesh, no?'

Simmy giggles. 'What a silly name for a robot.'

Sammy shrugs. 'It's just a man name. What happened to Dinesh, Ma?'

Ma sighs. 'It's a long story, but in a nutshell, Dinesh the Robot bolted from the containment area, and I had to physically tackle and stop it from escaping.'

Papa looks alarmed. 'That sounds dangerous. You could have gotten injured.'

Sammy looks at Ma proudly. 'That's amazing. Then what happened?'

Ma replies tiredly, 'The security alarm went off, the staff had to be evacuated, and the building went into lockdown.'

Simmy asks, 'But Ma, what was Dinesh escaping from? Did you torture him?'

Ma looks indignant. 'Of course not, Simmy. It was malfunctioning. The AI seems to have evolved so Dinesh is now developing a sense of self-awareness.'

'What does that mean?' the kids ask in unison. They look at each other and giggle. It is as if they have a secret code of communication that makes them speak the same words together sometimes.

'It just means Dinesh now has a mind of its own. It even said, while running out, "Bye bye! Off I go to the park!" I couldn't believe my ears.'

Sammy and Simmy burst out laughing.

Papa wasn't amused in the least. 'So you had to risk your life tackling a robot?'

Ma is annoyed. 'Don't be dramatic, Anil. There was no risk to my life. Anyway, my team members who were in the room managed to initiate a remote kill-switch to cut off its power.'

'All's well that ends well then,' Papa mutters sarcastically.

'Not really.' Ma snaps. 'We called a meeting of all the senior researchers. It's a scientific disaster. I really need to figure out what went wrong. As AI evolves, it changes in ways that we cannot predict. Everyone's worried. As am I.'

'As they should be.' Papa says grimly. 'Anyway, I was asking one of you to fetch me a glass of water, please.'

'Sammy, go, get a glass of water for your papa,' Ma says, looking at her game console screen again.

'Simmy, go, get a glass of water for your papa,' says Sammy.

'Woof,' says Bobby. She agrees with everyone. She loves her family very much.

Ma suddenly gets angry, as she often does. 'Enough,' she says, rather dramatically. 'So much fuss about a glass of water. It's my fault that both of you are ill-mannered but we will talk about that later. Now, just get up and fetch your father a glass of water.'

'Woof,' says Bobby, feeling left out. If only she had opposable thumbs.

'I can get it myself,' says Papa, a little sheepishly, 'Just that my back is hurting and . . .'

Sammy and Simmy look at each other. Papa is always complaining about something or the other, and Ma is always in a mood. Anyway, they don't want her to start shouting now.

They get up, and mumbling under their breath, head through the door into the corridor leading to the kitchen.

Bobby starts trotting down with them but changes her mind and comes back. She sits down with her head on Ma's lap. When Ma gets agitated, it is Bobby's job to calm her down.

As they shut the door, they hear Bobby whine quietly. Bobby is unnerved but no one pays her any attention or wonders why.

TWILIGHT ZONE 1

The corridor is a really short one, but today it seems to stretch a little. Sammy and Simmy don't notice this at first because they are busy commenting on how annoying their parents are.

They keep walking down the corridor till Sammy stops suddenly and says, 'Wait, Simmy. What is going on?'

Simmy looks at his sister and then at the corridor behind them. It is shimmering and hazy. His eyes feel dazzled.

Sammy is staring ahead. The corridor looks stretchy like it was made of play dough.

'We have to go forward, I think,' she says, thoroughly confused. She is the older one—she doesn't want Sammy to know she is clueless and suddenly very scared.

'I want to go back,' says Simmy, turning around. He takes a step towards the living room where his parents and Bobby are.

When he puts his foot out, it feels like being on an escalator, but going the wrong way. He can't move forward. Moving at all is hard, or rather, impossible.

Sammy and Simmy stand still.

'Maybe our eyes are playing tricks, or maybe Ma is doing something to teach us a lesson,' Sammy says.

'Yes,' agrees Simmy. 'She's always trying to teach us something or the other. Last week, she hid my geography workbook for twenty-four hours just because I kept leaving it all over the house and forgetting where it was. I couldn't do my homework and got a demerit in school.'

'Haha,' laughs Sammy, a little shakily. 'Ma is insane.'

'But I want Ma,' says Simmy, his voice suddenly all teary and wobbly.

'It's okay! She's there,' Sammy points in the direction of the living room.

But the corridor is so long and bright and shimmering now that she has to shut her eyes. 'Right there. We just need to get that glass of water and go back.'

'But I can't seem to go back, Sammy, I am trying so hard but I can't.' Simmy keeps trying to put a foot in the direction of the living room but that sense of riding an escalator the wrong way returns every time. It's impossible.

'Let's just go ahead and get that glass of water, okay?' Sammy says. She holds out her hand, and Simmy clutches it so hard that Sammy winces, but doesn't tick him off as she would have on a normal day.

Going forward is easy enough, they find. Like being on a walkalator. They move forward swiftly with no trouble whatsoever through the stretchy corridor, which looks like it is made of a rubbery green and dull orange plasticine.

The stretchy corridor keeps elongating in front of them, with no end in sight. They walk on, *a little like zombies*, Sammy thinks, with the single-minded aim of getting a glass of water for Papa.

Finally, after what feels like ten years (but might be just ten minutes or less), they find the kitchen door on the left, exactly where it is meant to be. It's a wooden door with the top half panelled with glass.

Sammy puts a hand on the doorknob as if in a dream. She looks through the glass and feels a rush of relief—it is their kitchen, it looks normal and cozy. Maybe they just imagined this whole lengthening and disappearing corridor rubbish.

She opens the door quickly and steps in, with Simmy still clutching her other hand. The door shuts behind them on its hinges, as always, with a small click.

But just as that click happens, the room expands. *Like zooming out on an image by gliding your fingers outward on a phone screen,* Sammy thinks.

The room is suddenly about four times larger than usual.

Sammy freezes, staring, not believing her eyes. Simmy, not letting go of his sister's hand, takes a step backward, peering out over her shoulder.

The kitchen stove and counters haven't changed, they are just much further away and there's a lot of floor space now. The glistening black-and-white floor tiles have expanded. The floor is like a giant chessboard, rimmed by kitchen counters, a double sink, a larder, a fridge and a gas oven with burners on top.

The fridge is where it's supposed to be, but it has expanded along with the floor and tiles. It's huge, taking up a lot of space from the floor to the ceiling and sideways too. It's a brand-new, steel-grey fridge that Papa loves, with double doors and many fancy new features. Sammy and Simmy had hardly paid any attention to it before, but now they are astonished by how gigantic it is—by how its gleaming, steely surface looks almost like a mirror.

They find themselves taking a slow step towards the fridge when they hear someone clearing their throat, just behind them.

It's Papa!

Sammy and Simmy have never felt so delighted to see their father ever before. They rush towards him and hug him as tightly as they can. They are so relieved to see him, so very happy!

Papa slowly but firmly holds their arms and pushes them away. Gently, but it's a strange thing for their loving Papa to do. They look up at his face in surprise.

Something is wrong. It is Papa, and it isn't.

Sammy and Simmy's hearts sink as they look at him. Their father is a kind man, but this Papa has a cruel look in his eyes that is impossible to miss. They look into Papa's eyes, mesmerized, and they know something is terribly wrong.

Is this really Papa? The eyes aren't his.

TWILIGHT ZONE 2

It's just in the eyes. A hint of meanness. Otherwise, he is Papa.

'Oh, come on, kiddos,' he says heartily.

Sammy and Simmy look at him warily. Their father has never greeted them with 'Oh, come on, kiddos' before.

'What's happening?' asks Sammy. She's still relieved they've found Papa, though something about him feels a little off. She also notices he's wearing a beach shirt with big, bright coconut trees, something she's never seen him wear before.

Papa takes out a pair of sunglasses from his pocket hurriedly, takes off his glasses and puts the sunglasses on, as if he had meant to earlier but forgotten.

'Aren't both of you here to get me water?' He laughs, though it really wasn't a joke.

'Go on then. Get me a glass of cold, cold water.'

Sammy and Simmy walk to the fridge. There is a cold water dispenser on the door but now that it has expanded so much, it almost looks like a waterfall.

Simmy grabs a glass from the counter next to the fridge. Thankfully, it's a normal-sized glass. He can feel Papa's eyes on him though he doesn't look at him as he takes the glass and holds it out in front of the dispenser. He has to lift his hand right above his head as the water dispenser is higher up than it used to be.

Water cascades down from the dispenser and hits the glass with a lot of force—like it's really coming from a waterfall. Simmy, standing on his toes with one hand stretched upwards, loses balance. The wet and slippery glass slips from his hand and crashes on to a black tile. There are shards of glass and water everywhere.

Simmy looks at his sister, who shakes her head and says, 'Never mind, Simmy. We'll clean it up.'

Sammy realizes she doesn't quite know how to clean up broken glass and looks at her father for help.

Papa is laughing silently, his belly wobbling, his double chin trembling. 'Not that easy to get a glass of water, is it?' he asks between giggles.

Some of the ice-cold water has splashed on Simmy. He feels wet and miserable. He asks his dad pleadingly, 'Can we just go home?'

Papa laughs so hard that he doubles over. 'Can we just go home?' he mimics Simmy, making his voice nasal and mean.

'But where are we, if not at home? Get that glass of water, will you now?'

Sammy whispers, 'Let's get a bottle from inside the fridge.' She pulls at the door which is big and heavy. Simmy joins her.

'NO,' Papa says. 'Don't open the door, get it from the dispenser please. As always.'

'No,' Sammy says, suddenly desperate to open the door in front of her. 'Simmy, pull. Put your hand around the side of the door and pull.'

'NO,' roars Papa. 'NOT THE DOOR.'

He starts taking long strides towards them.

The door makes a pop sound and opens. Sammy pushes Simmy inside so hard that he practically rolls in and throws herself in after him. The door shuts behind them smoothly just as they see Papa's hand reaching out to stop them.

'He's coming after us,' whispers Simmy.

'No, he can't. This is our room. He can't enter,' Sammy says calmly. She doesn't know how she knows they are in their bedroom, but she does.

TWILIGHT ZONE 3

It's dark at first. They blink a few times. Then, as if night turns into day in a matter of seconds, they can suddenly see. With immense relief, they realize they really are in their bedroom. The two study tables sit against one wall, beneath the bunk beds where they sleep. The ceiling is the same yolk-yellow as always, and the red carpet with green polka dots stretches across the floor.

Behind them, where they entered, there is now a smooth wall, just like it should be; the fridge door isn't there at all.

'But what is . . . what . . . I don't know what's going on?' Sammy flops down on a bean bag, feeling completely exhausted and frowns. 'Are you . . . are you okay, Simmy?'

'Where's Ma?' asks Simmy. He is feeling both relieved and anxious together, if that's even possible.

'And where's Papa, for that matter? THAT creature wasn't Papa,' Sammy says.

'But it was. He was just being weird . . . it seems.' Simmy falters, not sure of anything really.

Simmy looks like he's about to cry but doesn't say anything more. Sammy also falls silent. It doesn't matter whose fault it is but they need to figure out what's going on. She looks around the room carefully.

Yes, it is definitely their room. Nothing enlarged or weird here. The cupboard door is ajar with clothes piled all higgledy-piggledy on the shelves. Her keds are on the floor with the socks tucked inside, just the way she left them, right next to Simmy's badminton racquet, lying diagonally across the jute rug in front of the cupboard.

'Are we like safe now . . . like, really?' asks Simmy, clutching a big fluffy penguin which he has had since he was three. He always feels better when he holds Fluff the penguin.

'I think so. For the moment,' Sammy says thoughtfully.

Everything here is just the way it should be. She doesn't want to say this aloud and alarm Simmy, but she is not sure what they will find if they leave the room. She wants to be with Ma, to hear her tell them firmly that all this never happened.

But Papa? Was that man in the kitchen really Papa? She has a sinking feeling in her stomach. She knows this—whatever this is, whatever is happening—isn't over yet.

Simmy heads towards the bathroom.

'Where are you going?' Sammy asks rather sharply.

'Just to wash my face,' says Simmy, who likes to splash water on his face many times a day.

'You can't . . . I mean, I don't know . . . wait,' says Sammy. She doesn't quite know why, but she's suddenly filled with dread.

She follows her brother to the bathroom.

'What?' asks Simmy as he turns the bathroom door handle and steps in.

Sammy follows him. She has a very bad feeling about opening doors now and is not going to let her little brother go anywhere alone, even if it's only the bathroom.

'What are you doing, Sammy? I am just going to . . .' Simmy sounds a little exasperated as he turns around to look at his sister but then stops. He freezes at the horrified expression on her face.

The door has clicked shut behind them.

TWILIGHT ZONE 4

The bathroom has expanded just like the kitchen did.

   The room is huge with the patterned floor tiles stretched into big squares, the ceiling high up and far away. The sink, towel rack and commode are still along the wall, unchanged in size, but now looking small and distant because the room is so vast. Only the bathtub is huge—the way the fridge was in the kitchen. It appears like a swimming pool almost, filled nearly to the brim.

Both Simmy and Sammy take a step back towards the bathroom door; they want to get back into their own room quickly. They don't say anything to each other, but they know they need to leave. They don't know what will happen if they stay, but escape this room they must.

Before they can do anything though, a cheerful, high-pitched voice greets them. 'Hey kids!'

Ma comes out from one side of the bathroom which they couldn't see till now because it was hidden behind the enormous bathtub.

Sammy and Simmy both feel a moment of relief, but it evaporates just as fast.

Ma is wearing a short maroon pleated pencil skirt with a white frilly top tucked into it. It is not the sort of thing their mother wears. And she has on big rectangular spectacles with a light blue frame, but Ma didn't even wear specs.

Behind the specs her eyes are large and bulging. They remember how Papa's eyes had also changed in the kitchen and were all mean and unkind.

'We need to leave,' Simmy whispers, but when he turns towards the door, it's no longer there.

'What are you saying, my sweet petunia?' asks Ma in her new high-pitched voice.

My sweet petunia? This is not how Ma talks! The two look at each other as Ma says, 'Come, Simmy, don't you want to wash your face?'

'No,' says Simmy, as Ma heads towards the sink.

'Come, come,' Ma replies. 'What's the matter with you, you silly little boy?' she adds cheerily as Simmy presses against his sister and doesn't move.

'Into the bathtub,' Sammy whispers.

'What?' asks Simmy, bewildered.

'We need to get into the tub.' Sammy knows they need to do this. She is sure.

'I don't want to take a bath,' Simmy whimpers.

'What are you two doing *phusur phusur* about?' asks Ma. Her voice is still bright and loud but her lips are in a straight line now, and she looks displeased. 'Come here then, both of you.'

Sammy is taking sideways steps towards the bathtub, which is really more a swimming pool now. Simmy, clinging to her, follows. He is alarmed and wondering if his sister is losing her mind with all the strange things going on. *Why does Sammy suddenly feel they must take a bath?*

'Trust me, get in,' Sammy says as they reach the side of the tub.

'It's too high,' says Simmy, who is small for his age. The giant tub now rises higher than the top of his head.

'Jump,' Sammy urges, her voice tense. 'I'll help you.'

'What are you doing?' Ma's voice is sharp.

Sammy hoists Simmy up so he falls into the water with a splash.

'STOP!'

Ma charges towards Sammy, her face pinched and angry. She is wearing black stilettoes and can only take quick, small steps.

Sammy places her palms flat on the side of the tub and pushes herself up, in one fluid motion, into the water.

Ma lunges for Sammy's right foot as it blurs past her hand, but she is not fast enough. Sammy lands in the tub.

Ma is at the side of the tub now, screaming. Her voice is hoarse, and now that they can't see her, they realize it isn't Ma's voice at all.

'Come out right now,' she says, or rather the fake-Ma voice says.

Sammy and Simmy see her hands appear around the rim of the tub. Her nails are bright pink, sharp and manicured—though Sammy remembers Ma complaining this very morning about her chipped nails, and saying she needs to file them and put some polish.

The hands gripping the rim of the tub are tightening, getting a firmer hold as Ma prepares to hoist herself up. They can see her forehead and large bulging eyes behind the glasses over the rim too. Her forehead is puckered and there are frown lines between her brows.

'What do we do?' Simmy asks. The bottom of the tub seems to have dropped away, and they are both treading water.

'Let's swim downwards,' Sammy says, and they quickly flip over and start swimming down and down and down.

As they keep swimming deeper and deeper towards the bottom of the tub which seems to never come, they find themselves tumbling on to a floor. The water whooshes away and recedes into the ceiling.

TWILIGHT ZONE 5

They are back in their bedroom. Their safe place. They look at each other. They have no idea what's happening, but at least they are back in their room.

'We aren't even wet,' says Simmy wonderingly, touching his shirt and his arms. He looks at his sister. She is bone dry too. 'We were in the bathtub, we swam underwater . . .'

'Yes yes,' says Sammy. 'I was there. We need to figure what is going on. The physical manifestations are clearly unimportant.'

'Physical manifestations?' Simmy asks. He can tell his sister is using Ma's language, the sort of thing she says when explaining the immersive games she creates. 'You think Ma is behind this?'

'I feel very sure she is,' Sammy says grimly, trying to get the image of the bathroom mother out of her head. Their own mother is the one she trusts—if she's behind this, they are safe. She knows it.

'Ma wouldn't do this to us,' Simmy's voice is shaky. 'This is terrifying.'

Sammy frowns. That's true. Ma can be annoying but what they've been going through has been seriously bizarre. How can this be Ma's doing? She wishes it is, but Ma is not cruel. What has been happening to them is horrid and cruel.

'Suppose we didn't get out through the fridge or the bathtub?' Simmy adds. 'If we hadn't managed to escape . . . we don't know what would've happened.'

'True,' says Sammy. 'But we did get away, so perhaps we were meant to.'

The two of them are still huddled in the middle of the room, right where they landed after swimming out of the bathtub.

They look around the room. The door to their bedroom that leads down the corridor to the living room looks the way it is meant to—a regular panelled brown door. They are both looking at that door now, fearfully but with longing. After all, their parents and Bobby are supposed to be in the living room.

'Let's just go into the living room?' Simmy says, though he sounds scared. Suppose things go awfully wrong again? They will be left with nothing. If they can't find their actual parents, there will be no escape from this nightmare.

Sammy is having the same thoughts.

'Should we just . . . you know, open the closet door instead?' she suggests. 'Just to see . . .'

They have a large closet in their room. The double door to the closet is big, twice the size of the main bedroom door really.

'The closet is a little open already, Sammy,' Simmy says slowly.

Some clothes are sticking out of the door, and it is ajar. Perhaps they can safely open that door and see what happens. Like a test drive before braving the door to the corridor.

'Or should we just try to go to the living room as you were saying,' Sammy says, suddenly longing for her parents again. Her normal, regular parents. Her mother, who scolds them a little too much, and her father, who's always whining about this and that.

They get up. Their legs feel shaky. They look at the cupboard door. They look at the door to the living room.

Which door should they open?

TWILIGHT ZONE 6

Sammy is feeling warrior-like.

'We aren't babies,' she says. 'We can do this. We are not going to wait for anyone to save us!'

She feels good when Simmy looks at her with something like respect in his eyes. It is new. He is not used to her taking charge. Ma often complains that Sammy behaves as if they are twins, not like the older sister she is.

'Yes we can!' Simmy agrees bravely. Then his expression wavers. 'But . . . hmm . . . umm . . . how? And what is it we are trying to do?'

'Our house is acting strange, our parents are acting strange—we need to figure out what's going on. Make the house behave, make Ma and Papa behave.'

'Except we don't know how,' Simmy adds.

'Instinct. Guesswork. We've known how to get away both the times—somehow. So, let's get on with it.' Sammy feels confident.

'But luck can run out.' Simmy doesn't feel as confident as his sister.

'It's not just luck. I've really known what needs to be done and been very sure about it.' Sammy is feeling a little irritated with her little brother. She has got him out of the kitchen and bathroom successfully. He needs to trust her a little more.

'The cupboard door is ajar, Sammy. It might not work in the same way as opening a closed door,' Simmy says.

'Yes,' agrees Sammy. 'Maybe it being open will help in some way though—undo something and make everything go back to normal.'

Sammy isn't at all sure if what she's saying makes any sense, but she and Simmy high-five at the very idea of things going back to normal.

The cupboard is large with two panelled teakwood doors that meet in the middle, each with a handle on either side. They walk up to the doors, stand in front of them, and look at each other. Sammy peers through the gap without touching the door.

'We can't really go in,' she says. 'There are shelves. There is more space where the clothes are hanging, but it would be weird to go and sit inside a cupboard, wouldn't it?'

Without saying another word, they each grab a handle and pull the doors open at the same time. Sometimes, they don't need to speak to each other to know what to do.

Sammy and Simmy are still standing in their own room, in their safe space. But they are staring into the cupboard which has expanded into a dream toyshop of sorts. The shelves are set back, out of reach from where they stand, but they're packed tightly with toy cars, dolls, teddies and board games, some still wrapped in cellophane. Simmy notices the kitchen set that they tried to convince Papa to buy for them but he said it's too expensive. The large paintbox with sixty-four tubes of paint and four brushes that he has been coveting for ages is also there.

However, it's not like the cupboard has expanded. Unlike what happened in the case of the kitchen and the bathroom, the cupboard is no longer simply a cupboard. It is a place of magic and beauty. The shelves are placed in an inky blue sky with puffs and wisps of clouds and twinkling stars.

It is too enchanting to resist.

Sammy and Simmy take a step forward, placing one foot each inside the cupboard, the other still planted in the safety of their bedroom. They look at each other.

TWILIGHT ZONE 7

The moment they cross the threshold, a weightlessness creeps up their legs. The foot inside the cupboard feels very light but it's also firmly placed—like it's pressing down on something that isn't there. They look down, expecting floorboards, but their feet are resting on nothing—on air, really. Their stomachs lurch. The cupboard has no bottom, just like the bathtub.

'We can step in. It's just that we will not be standing on the ground, more like in the sky, in air, sort of,' Simmy says. His voice sounds a little faraway to Sammy, as if it's coming through a tunnel. She doesn't have a good feeling about this.

'Perhaps we shouldn't go in?' she says, but her words are blown away and scattered, and Simmy doesn't really hear her.

Besides, he is staring at the paintbox that he wants. He is drawn towards it and steps into the cupboard or really, into the starry, cloudy night sky that is patterned with the shelves brimming with toys and books.

Sammy sighs. Despite the growing feeling of unease that she has, she follows him in. She is relieved that the door doesn't click shut behind them this time—possibly because it was already ajar.

It is beautiful inside, velvety and dark with stars glittering like sparkly diamonds and soft powdery clouds twirling around lazily. Simmy is striding ahead towards the paintbox. She follows reluctantly. The shelves recede, they are moving back, deeper into the night sky.

Sammy says, 'Simmy, the shelves are shifting, moving out of reach. I think we shouldn't be here.'

'You go back if you want, Sammy,' Simmy says in a hoarse, cold voice, turning to look at his sister. His face has changed. Against the dark sky, his skin is chalky white. She can see that his eyes are cold and green—not brown-black like they're meant to be—and his lips twist into a cruel smile that doesn't reach his eyes.

Sammy's heart sinks—she literally feels it somersault and drop in her chest. *This can't be happening*, she tells herself as she takes a step back.

The distance between brother and sister lengthens. Sammy can't tear her eyes away from Simmy's twisted face. She wants to escape, the way she escaped the strange versions of Ma and Papa, but this is Simmy. How can she leave without him?

Just the other day, Sammy had twisted Simmy's arm because he had snatched and gobbled the last chicken nugget from her plate. Simmy had cried out in pain and Ma had said, 'Sammy, really—your little brother! You should be looking after him, not twisting his arm and making him cry.'

Sammy had felt it was awful of Ma to take Simmy's side when he was the one who had acted greedy and then stuck his tongue out at her when Ma wasn't looking. But those words come back to her now. This is her little brother, and she needs to look after him. He is only eight. She can't leave him alone here.

Sammy stands inside the cupboard or in the night sky, depending on how one wants to see it. In any case, whatever it may be, she knows she needs to get away. Her feet urge her to run—back into the room, into the safe space.

She whispers, 'Simmy, why are you . . .'

'Why am I what?' Simmy's voice is loud, hoarse and unfamiliar. He continues walking towards the paintbox that he wants but turns his head around to look at Sammy. His skin looks papery and wrinkled, like someone much older.

Sammy feels a chill run down her back but she doesn't want to leave. Instead, she says, 'You don't need the paintbox, Simmy. Let's just go back.'

'I need it. I want it,' Simmy says in a greedy voice. 'You go away, scaredy-cat.'

'No,' Sammy says firmly as Simmy reaches for the paintbox. She rushes up to him and grabs his hand before he can touch the paintbox. She pulls at his shirt and pushes him back, repeating, 'No, no.'

They both stumble backwards.

Sammy looks at her little brother fearfully. She has no idea how he will react now.

Simmy's face is expressionless. The wrinkles fade, and his eyes are shut. Sammy grips his hand tightly and begins dragging him toward the cupboard door. He doesn't resist, but he also doesn't help her. He simply allows her to do what she wants.

Sammy pulls him towards the door and pushes him hard, so he lands in the room with a thud. She follows him into the room and kneels beside him.

He looks like himself again, except that his eyes are a little dazed. She hugs him and says, 'Are you okay, Simmy? What happened?'

'I don't know, I'm feeling a little pukey, but I'm fine,' Simmy replies in his normal voice. Sammy heaves a sigh of relief.

The cupboard doors have clicked shut behind them. It looks like a normal closet in a normal room. Not at all like one that could be holding the sky and the stars inside it.

Sammy sighs again. If only they could be back in the living room with Ma and Papa.

IN THE LIVING ROOM 1

Back in the living room, there is chaos. Bobby is barking and scampering around. Ma is on her phone, talking to her boss, Kamila Motorwala. She has been on the call for a while now, pacing up and down, telling Kamila how the children disappeared, growing more and more frantic. Sometimes, she even trips over Bobby.

Only Papa is still. He sits with his head buried in his hands.

'We have reached. Coming right in,' Kamila says from just outside the door and rings the bell.

Bobby rushes to the door and breaks into a fresh frenzy of barks. Papa opens the door, and Kamila, Aayan and Manohar enter.

Aayan, the head of the research wing at the EIGDC, has a habit of pulling his left ear with his right hand when distressed. He is doing it now. Manohar, head of the technology wing, follows close behind.

'I really don't understand what is going on.' Ma is still speaking on the phone.

'You can put the phone down, ma'am. We are with you now,' Manohar says soothingly. 'I mean, don't worry. We will figure this out.'

Ma stops mid-sentence, puts the phone down and glares at him. 'My children have been caught in the maze for an hour now, and you still haven't figured out what needs to be done?'

'What is this maze-maze you keep saying?' Papa asks. He has heard Ma say it on the phone many times, but each time he's asked what she means, she has only said, 'Wait, wait,' and never explained.

'This has never happened before, you know that, Damini,' Kamila says. 'And you know you shouldn't be bringing your console home. It isn't safe.'

'I don't care,' Ma screams, forgetting that Kamila is her boss who she respects and cares for. 'Just get them out.'

Kamila stays calm. Aayan and Manohar try to hide their shock at seeing Damini ma'am in this state. Her hair is all over the place, her kajal is smudged, her sari crumpled and slipping off her shoulder. But her children have gone missing, so it's hardly surprising that she's hot, bothered and a complete mess.

Kamila walks towards the game console which is lying on the dining table. She looks at the map of the house on the screen. It is like an architect's blueprint, neat lines, all labelled—living room, kitchen, children's room, master bedroom, guest room, study and bathrooms 1, 2 and 3.

Papa wipes his tears, steps behind Kamila and scowls at the screen.

Aayan puts a hand on his shoulder and mutters, 'Don't worry, sir. It will be okay.'

'I just don't understand,' Papa says, blinking back his tears. 'Damini hasn't told me what's going on.'

'I hear you,' Kamila says grimly but not taking her eyes off the screen. She clicks on a button and the screen is now 3D. It no longer looks like a simple architect's map. They have a bird's eye view of the house. The walls are marked by thick double lines, the rooms are miniature versions of the actual rooms in the house with furniture and curtains and rugs. Like an open-plan dollhouse viewed from above. Except it is their home, the one they've lived in for ten years.

And except for the fact that the living room—where they are right now—is missing from the map. The house starts from the door which leads to the corridor, as if the house is suddenly one room short.

'Can someone *please* tell me what is going on?' Papa asks, glaring at the screen.

'Where are Sammy and Simmy? And why is the living room not on the map?'

'Mazes and labyrinths. We are developing an immersive game where a house can become a live maze that you have to find your way out of. It uses AI to tap into the player's deepest fears, so the game is different for everyone who plays it. The research phase is almost complete, but the game is far from ready for trial,' Kamila says, glaring at Damini. 'We aren't supposed to be working on it at home at all.'

Damini looks petrified and defiant at the same time. 'I had no idea it could suddenly start up and endanger the lives of my children . . . Because of what happened with Dinesh today, I wanted to . . . '

Before she can complete the sentence Papa butts in, 'Endanger? What do you mean? We are talking about our children—who have been missing for more than an hour now, disappeared from under our noses, in our own house—and all you fools can do is talk of trials and deepest fears?'

Under normal circumstances, Papa, a very polite person, would never have called his wife and her colleagues fools. But now he is beside himself with anger and fear. He is angriest with Ma. God knows what she's been up to, and she hasn't bothered to explain anything to him at all.

'Calm down, Anil,' Ma says to Papa as if she hasn't been screaming and shouting for the past hour. 'In a nutshell, we are developing a game that allows people—adults and kids over twelve—to experience their own homes like a maze. It's quite mind-bogglingly exciting really—combining AI and psychology in ways that never have been used ever. The game uses the player's environment and adapts based on the player's mental state. The mind plays an important role here—what you see as your safe space, what you fear can go wrong, is simulated by AI to push the players to find their way out of the maze.'

'And what does this have to do with Simmy and Sammy?' Papa asks as quietly as he can.

'Well, I was working on the game at home, and I think I accidentally activated some setting that pulled the kids into the game,' Ma says, wringing her hands and shaking her head apologetically. 'They're inside the maze now, but they have no idea they're playing. They can't be knowing that they're in a game. The environment is real to them. I'm sorry but I'm not sure how they are navigating the maze. As we've seen till now, Anil, we can't seem to leave this room except through the main door and the rest of the house is . . . inaccessible. The corridor to the kitchen is no longer accessible; the door is just fused.'

'Technology gone rogue . . . I've told you! How many times have I told you that whatever you do, the work you do, is dangerous?' Papa is furious. 'And as for that door, shall I call a carpenter?'

'I don't think a carpenter can help,' Kamila says calmly.

'I am so sorry,' says Ma and bursts into tears.

Everyone falls silent.

Ma finally stops and blows her nose noisily. She looks at Manohar and Kamila, a mix of relief and desperation in her eyes. 'How can we fix it?'

'Well, the trial version could have just accidentally started,' begins Manohar, when Papa interrupts.

'Can't you just get them out if it is the trial version?'

'There is no ESCAPE button, and you can't pull them out. There is no way for me to hardcode it now. They just have to work their way throught the maze,' Manohar replies.

'What worries me most is their psychological state,' Kamila says. 'How are the kids coping with their fears? Are they playing the same game? Their fears won't be the same, will they?'

'They should be able to work their way out, don't worry. It's just that they should not be too scared—that wouldn't be good for them,' Aayan says.

Ma and Papa look at each other. *Should be able to work their way out. They shouldn't be too scared.* None of it sounds reassuring.

'I won't be surprised if they have similar fears, since they are in this together,' Ma says, trying to persuade herself. 'There is a two-year age gap between them, but they are very close. Sometimes, they really operate like twins.'

'That's good,' Aayan says. 'It means they are also looking out for each other. In a fearful situation, that bond helps—they'll be brave for each other.'

'We can't be sure,' Papa says. He isn't sure he understands any of it himself either. 'How is this even a game? A maze? I don't know.'

'You know, sir, maze video games have been around for more than fifty years now. You know . . .' Aayan starts. He has a habit of launching into long lectures.

'I don't need a history lesson on video games. I want to know how to reach my kids, wherever they are,' Papa snaps. He thinks he is beginning to understand what is happening, as bizarre as it sounds.

'I was just explaining sir,' says Aayan, pulling his left ear with his right hand. He is upset at how rude Papa is being when he's only trying to explain what's going on. 'What makes this different is that it uses AI, so the player is truly inside the game. AI determines the environments they find themselves in—more than our coding does. Your kids will surely get out, but the question is how to get them out quickly and without any harm.'

'It's a very intricate, complicated design—this game. Going to take the world by storm,' Manohar says, proudly.

'How dare you? I will sue all of you. I will make sure this game is never made,' Papa is shouting now.

Manohar looks alarmed. Kamila shoots Manohar a disapproving look. He doesn't say much, but often says the wrong things when he does.

'Let me just track the children now. It is impossible to change anything because it is governed by AI, but we can track how many players there are and where they are. Then we can figure out what can be done,' Kamila says soothingly.

She taps on the keyboard and pushes the two buttons on either side of the keyboard. Suddenly, the whole house appears on the screen.

Two figures appear in the children's room—miniature figures of a boy and a girl.

'Ah, there they are,' she says triumphantly.

Papa and Ma's faces brighten. They feel the tension of the last couple of hours ease a little. They look at the two miniature figures on the screen with love and longing. They want to hug and hold their children and reassure them that something like this will never happen again.

But the moment is shattered when Kamila adds, 'We can see them, but not help them, I am afraid.'

Papa glares at her and is about to say something when Kamila holds up a hand to stop him.

'As Aayan was trying to explain before you stopped him—mostly all video games are linear and programmed. But this one isn't programmed in that sense. It is AI that makes all the decisions. It tracks the house and creates the maze. Because the game itself is procedurally generated, the only way to get out of the game . . . is by actually finishing it.'

IN THE LIVING ROOM 2

The miniature figures move towards the cupboard and are about to enter it.

Everyone in the living room watched anxiously.

The figures disappear, and all they can see now are two dots inside the cupboard. The dots pulsate slowly but do not move.

As the minutes pass, their tension levels rise steadily.

'What are they doing?' Papa bursts out.

'We have no way of knowing,' Manohar replies. There's no way to monitor what's happening inside.

Then the dots disappear from the cupboard.

Everyone gasps.

After a moment which seems like an hour, two miniature figures reappear in their room.

Everyone heaves a sigh of relief. Bobby lies down with her head between her paws and lets out a deep sigh.

'Your kids are brilliant,' Kamila gushes. 'Don't know how they are doing this—getting out every time. Clearly, they are solving whatever challenges they are facing.'

'But you people still have no idea what's actually going on, do you?' Papa says rudely.

Kamila doesn't mind. She is just relieved that the kids seem to be doing okay. A dotted trail on the screen shows that they've already been inside the kitchen, the bathroom and now the cupboard—and each time, they've returned to their room. That is an excellent sign.

Aayan states, 'They are smart kids! Are you sure you don't want to lower the minimum age to eight, Damini ma'am? Bigger market.'

Papa and Ma glare at him, and even Manohar seems to realize that this is not the right thing to say.

Kamila looks at her watch. Ma is also aware that the clock is ticking. It's reassuring that the kids seem to be holding up well, but for how long? They need to get them out.

'Let me take a look, Kamila ma'am,' says Manohar.

The others are more familiar with the design and concepts, but he knows the technology best—the mechanics of how the game actually works.

Kamila gets up, and Manohar takes her place. They crowd around him. Aayan puts his hand on Manohar's shoulder and leans over to peer at the screen.

'Can all of you . . . if you don't mind . . .' Manohar swallows.

'Yes, yes,' Kamila says, taking a step back. 'Let him concentrate, everyone. Let him be. No pressures, Manoharji. Do your thing.'

Aayan takes his hand off and moves away, pulling his left ear with his right hand sadly.

'I mean, there has to be some other way,' Manohar mutters to himself. 'I mean . . . not possible, no?'

'Why isn't it possible?' Papa says. 'To exit a game, one should be able to close the app. And if the kids aren't able to do that because . . . hmm . . . they don't have the controls, then you should be able to close it from here.'

'We can, in theory,' Ma agrees. 'It's just that it is not really an option in a game like this. And if we do, who knows?'

'Who knows what?' Papa asks. 'I wish y'all would stop talking in riddles.'

Ma takes a deep breath. 'See, Anil. We haven't finished developing the game, as you have understood too, right? There are gaps in the code. So yes, it is possible to escape—but we don't know what will happen to the kids if they do.'

'Why?' asks Papa. 'As far as I know when I press the ESCAPE button, I escape a game. *Bas*. That's all. *Khatam*.'

'This does not have an ESCAPE button, Anil,' Ma says patiently.

'I mean, in this kind of immersive game, there are no pre-defined levels. The game doesn't just load one environment after another. It's dynamic. The AI is constantly generating content based on player interaction and decision-making—basically, procedural generation,' Manohar interjects, not looking up from the screen.

Papa looks even more confused.

'Right,' Kamila adds. 'When the kids make choices, the game is adapting and changing the layout of the house as they see it, the maze itself, as they go along.'

Ma continues, 'And don't you find sometimes when you haven't finished a game, not gone through all the levels or whatever and you press the ESCAPE key, you find yourself back at the beginning, of that level or of the game itself. You know, like restart . . .'

'Umm, yes, sure, but even then . . . you can give it a shot. If it doesn't work, then we can see . . . If this is our best shot, then we should try it, no?' Papa insists.

'The children are part of the game, Anil. We don't know what ending the game forcibly will do to their minds,' Kamala says.

Manohar grunts in frustration, and they all turn around to look at him.

'I am trying to get into the source code,' he says, 'but AI keeps throwing me out.'

'What do you mean?' Ma asks. Then it dawns on her, 'Oh, the AI . . .'

'Yes,' says Manohar, 'the AI thinks I am a hacker trying to manipulate the game, so it keeps locking me out.' He waves them away and says, 'Let me work.'

'So how is this game supposed to end if the AI keeps changing things and you have no control?' asks Papa.

'This ending is a very cool new feature we've introduced, how and where the game ends is determined by the player,' Ma says.

'The player can only get out through their own actions.'

'What actions are these?' demands Papa.

'They have to take a leap of courage. There is no predetermined step. It has to be something that the AI cannot predict, which is so counterintuitive that it baffles AI's algorithms,' says Kamila.

Ma says, 'Can you imagine what might happen if it restarts? They'll have to play it again, go back to the beginning—they'll be caught in an infinite loop.'

'Yes,' Kamila says grimly. 'You don't know what impact it will have on their psyches, their minds, if they find themselves caught in an infinite loop.'

'We need to track the game's memory and look at the player states,' Manohar says, his fingers flying over the keyboard. 'If we see that, we can to figure out how close they are to the end. But I can't seem to access the main code. The system is blocking me.'

Papa exhales furiously. The rest of them look at each other helplessly.

TWILIGHT ZONE 8

For the past half hour, Sammy and Simmy have been sitting rather quietly, huddled together on one bean bag. They are still recovering from the cupboard experience.

Simmy is trying to get the image of Sammy's cruel green eyes out of her head. They both glance at the cupboard and bathroom doors a few times. Both the doors are firmly shut. They are at a loss—not sure what they should do now.

Sammy wants to reassure Simmy that they will be fine, but finds that she no longer has the words for it. She doesn't feel very fine herself. She's finding it harder to breathe; the air in the room feels stale.

Next to the bathroom door, there's a small window that looks out on to the backyard. The checked curtains are always drawn because it has no view—just a walled-in yard with a dirt floor. Papa had put up a swing in the yard when they were younger, but it broke.

Sammy gets up and draws the curtains.

Simmy jumps up, 'What are you doing, Sammy?'

Sammy stops in her tracks and looks at him, suddenly worried. 'I was going to open the window so the room gets some fresh air, but . . . should I not?'

Simmy stares at her. 'We could try. It's a window . . . it's for looking out, not for going into another room or the corridor or anything.'

They look at each other with excitement. Perhaps they will finally be able to get out. A window, after all, opens outwards—not into another room.

They stand in front of the window and draw the curtains back. All they can see is the mossy cement wall and the brown dirt floor outside. The yard is empty, except for the rope that had once held the swing. Papa had removed the wooden plank of the swing when it broke, but the rope is still there on the yard floor, surrounded by some straggly plants with sparse leaves and no flowers.

Sammy and Simmy reach out to open the glass windowpanes, their eyes fixed on the yard. As the panes swing open, a strong, cold gust of wind rushes into the room.

'Climb on to the sill—quick, Sammy!' Simmy is already clambering up and over into the yard. Sammy follows, and they're soon standing on the other side of the window.

The dust is swirling hard now, lashing sharply against their cheeks and necks. The yard darkens. The straggly plants have suddenly grown into tall tangled shrubs and trees.

'It's a jungle,' says Simmy wonderingly.

Sammy reaches out to hold his hand and says, 'Let's explore.'

Sammy's voice sounds different, older, like Ma's voice. It comforts Simmy.

They are deep inside a forest. Far off, Simmy hears the laugh of a hyena.

A few more steps, and in front of him he sees a thick coiled snake, which shifts a little, as if waking up. Its skin is scaly and glossy, as if the snake has just had an oil bath.

Simmy is filled with cold dread. He tries to tell Sammy they need to go back to their room, but no sound comes out. The snake's eyes are small and round but glitter so

brightly that Simmy blinks a few times. He is mesmerized, unable to look away, staring into those small, bottomless little holes.

'It's going to strike,' he finally manages to squeak, as the snake raises its hooded head, its forked tongue flickering in and out.

Sammy pats him on his head and says in Ma's voice, 'I don't think so . . . it just looks like it's a snake but . . .' She steps forward and bends down to touch the snake.

Simmy screams loudly, his body stiff with fear, his eyes squeezed shut.

'Look,' Sammy says.

Simmy opens his eyes to see they are no longer in the jungle, and Sammy is holding the old coiled rope of the swing. He's relieved, but the mossy, uncemented brick walls on three sides now seem to be closing in on them.

'Can we just go back to our safe room?' he whispers, his face pale, his eyes large like a raccoon's in his tiny face. The window through which they came out is, thankfully, still open.

Sammy doesn't seem to share his fear, but she looks disappointed. 'Yes, there's nothing here. Let's go back into the room. This is a dead end.'

She's right. The walled yard has no exit. The narrow passage that's supposed to connect their backyard to the front part of the house has disappeared.

Sammy and Simmy return to the room, shut the window and draw the curtains. They are hungry and thirsty as they flop down on to the bean bags in the middle of the room.

Sammy feels time slipping away. How long can this go on? There are no windows or doors left to explore. What can they do now, except sit and wait to be rescued? But who is going to save them?

She no longer has faith in the adults in her life. They can't sit and do nothing. They need to act.

TWILIGHT ZONE 9

'We have one more door left to open,' Simmy says. 'And it leads into the corridor and back to the living room.'

They look at each other helplessly. They remember how the corridor had stretched ahead of them, pulling them toward the kitchen. If they enter it now, they might be forced to go there again.

'I feel . . .' Sammy begins when Simmy clutches her hand and says, 'Look.'

'What?' asks Sammy.

'The bedroom door . . . it flashed a little,' Simmy says. 'But now it has . . . stopped.'

Sammy looks at her brother, worried. How can a door flash? Perhaps they will both slowly go mad and that's how this will all end.

She keeps an eye on the door, but nothing happens.

Until suddenly, it happens again.

'Yes, Simmy! It flashed! Green and orange lights,' Sammy shouts.

They both jump to their feet. But the door is back to behaving like an ordinary door. That is, it's up to nothing.

Minutes pass, they aren't sure how many. It feels like hours.

And then, it happens again. The door is bathed in a strange neon light, with green and orange streaks shooting across it haphazardly. They step towards it and hear a familiar sound that seems far away, but they know what it is.

Bobby is barking.

Sammy and Simmy look at each other excitedly. But what follows the barking is silence—sudden deep silence. It's like someone has gagged Bobby. A total silence falls, unlike anything they've ever experienced before. It's eerie.

'Let's open the door,' Simmy whispers. Sammy is filled with misgivings, but Simmy feels certain. He holds his sister's hand and says, 'Come.'

The door is still bathed in the neon light and the green and orange streaks are moving across it slowly, like lazy railway tracks and green fields from the window of a slow-moving train. It opens as Simmy turns the handle—or rather seems to melt away. So now there is a door-shaped hole leading into the corridor.

The corridor too is bathed in neon light, and the green and orange stripes are shooting around on the walls. But the walls look firm and solid—not stretchy and weird.

As they stand at the threshold of their room, the green and orange stripes start moving faster on the corridor walls, getting more frenzied with every passing second.

Then they hear a growl.

It's a menacing sound—low and deep. It rises, fills the air. It's a roar now.

The unmistakable roar of a lion.

Sammy and Simmy had been to the local zoo with their parents recently. The lion had been in a bad mood that day. He had come up to the bars of his cage and roared loudly. It had been scary—the sound had resonated all around them.

But now, alone in their room—not on a zoo visit—it's a million times scarier. They are lost and miserable, with no idea where Ma and Papa are. Though, really, who knows if they would've been able to help? With a lion about to spring on them, the situation feels as dire as it could get.

Simmy tugs at Sammy's hand and whispers, 'Let's step into the corridor.'

'This is a nightmare. I can't move,' Sammy says. They've had too many misadventures. Sammy wants to just give up. Her feet feel like lead.

'Come, Sammy. We need to go,' Simmy whispers urgently, pulling his sister into the corridor.

The lion—or whatever creature it is—roars again. Sammy looks at Simmy who puts his index finger on his lips and says, 'Shhh'.

Stillness, deep and empty, fills the air again. Then there is the sound of padded feet.

The lion is coming towards them. Down the corridor which has lengthened again but the walls aren't elastic or stretchy this time. It's a long, long prison-like corridor down which the lion is coming on padded feet.

It is moving slowly. It's a speck in the distance to begin with.

But Sammy and Simmy are inside the claustrophobic, deep, cage-like corridor with no iron bars separating them from the lion.

Sammy catches a whiff of a strong, foul smell—one she remembers from the lion's cage. It had made her feel nauseous that day at the zoo. She feels the bile rise in her throat and swallows, to stop herself from puking. The stench is filling the air. She desperately wants to go back into their room. It is their safe space. She wants to say this to Simmy but finds she has lost her voice. No words come out of her terrified throat.

She tugs at Simmy's hand, but Simmy is just looking ahead. His gaze is steady. He takes a few steps ahead towards the lion as if he is mesmerized.

The lion, which was moving slowly at first, is now picking up speed. A growl rumbles through the corridor again.

The lion is getting larger and larger, almost filling the corridor as it roars and springs towards them.

IN THE LIVING ROOM 3

'Manoharji, stop,' Kamila says suddenly.

Manohar looks up at her.

'Look there. That door was shimmering just now. There were these lights flashing on it. I don't know why.'

Everyone turns to look in the direction she's pointing.

'That's the glass door which leads to the corridor. We couldn't get through it. That's why we weren't able to go in and look for the kids,' Papa says excitedly.

They all nod solemnly.

Bobby whines and looks up. She had sniffed at the door earlier, but nothing had happened.

Now, the flashing lights are gone.

Manohar nods. A little uncertainly. He quickly types a series of commands into the console and all of them cry out.

The glass is shimmering in the shape of a big rectangle. Green and orange streaks flash across it. It now resembles a holographic, digital cutout, right where the corridor used to be.

Bobby gets up and rushes to the door. She whines, pawing at it desperately. The green and orange streaks become deeper, every time he scratches at the wall.

'I'm almost in!' Manohar yells in triumph.

Everyone turns to him, hopefully.

'That is excellent, Manoharji! What do we have to do?' Kamila asks.

'There is a password,' says Manohar. 'Somehow, when this game got launched, there was a developer password set. What is it?'

'A password?' splutters Papa.

The rest of them are looking at each other and shaking their heads worriedly.

'My children are stuck just because none of you know the password?'

Manohar replies, 'To access the code, we need the password. I mean, what is the password you set, Damini ma'am?'

'What password?' Ma shouts. 'I didn't set any password. You *know* I didn't.'

'You did.' Manohar glares at her as if she is deliberately refusing to save her kids. 'You really did. There is an error on the screen. I can exit the game safely for the kids, if only you say the password out loud.'

'What are you even saying, Manoharji? I have no idea,' Ma says, her eyes brimming with tears.

Meanwhile, Bobby flings herself against the door. It shimmers and glows. For a second, they catch a glimpse of the corridor but then it disappears again. Bobby whines and scampers back to lick Ma's hand.

'She has set a password. She really has,' Manohar is looking at Kamila and Aayan and ignoring Ma now. He takes a quick look at Papa, who is once again sitting with his head in his hands.

'Damini, you have set a password without realizing it,' Kamila says to her calmly, patting her back. 'Think, think. What could it be?'

'The trial mode of the game is triggered by voice activation. And since the system is unstable, it took a random password it identified because it was repeated thrice. There must be a word or phrase you said three times before the kids entered the corridor, Damini ma'am. That's what opened the portal, the corridor, and they entered the game,' Manohar says without looking in Ma's direction. 'If she doesn't remember it, then the kids will be locked in for god knows how many more hours.'

'They have no food, no water, nothing,' Papa says. 'And the door . . . it's fused again. Thank god it's stopped flashing in that strange way now.'

'I mean, even if I can access the main code with the password, then hopefully I can figure out how to end it,' Manohar says.

'You think? My children's lives?' says Papa, getting more and more annoyed.

'I don't know. The AI might still fight me.'

'Then I will go in. Open it . . . I'll go in. I'm sure I will be able to get them out. Really.' Papa refuses to sit there doing nothing if they manage to open up the corridor.

'It might not serve any purpose, you going in—supposing you even can. When the game began, it was probably set to two players. That's why only the children were pulled into the game. If you try to enter now, the game might just treat you as an NPC, a non-player character—an additional, irrelevant variable. You will just get stuck in there, Anil. I'm sorry. We can't force them to leave the game environment. The game's logic doesn't work like that—it's designed to be self-guided. They have to actively interact with the exit condition themselves,' Kamila says sadly.

'How will they interact with the exit condition when they don't know what the exit condition is?' demands Papa.

Ma has tears rolling down her cheeks now. She has no memory of setting a password. Her mind is blank and terrified.

Aayan sits down next to Ma. He isn't pulling his left ear with his right hand anymore. He knows it's important for all of them to be positive and calm. '*Arrey*, don't panic, Damini ma'am,' he says. 'We're almost there. You just need to retrace your steps from before the kids left this room. There is some word or phrase you repeated thrice while working on your console that activated the game. Think what it could have been.'

'Yes, Damini. Anil, you too. Both of you try to remember the sequence of events leading to the kids leaving the room,' Kamila says.

'Okay.' Papa looks at Kamila. 'My back was hurting, the kids were acting up and Damini got annoyed.'

'What did she say when she was annoyed?' Kamila asks.

'I mean, she has to have said it three times. The password could have been set only if she said a sequence of words three times.' Manohar looks visibly irritated by Damini's unreliable memory. They were almost there and now this. Too much.

'Anil wanted a glass of water, and the kids were fussing and not getting it for him,' Ma says slowly, trying to recall exactly what had happened. 'I was working on the game but got really annoyed and ordered them to go and get a glass of water.' Her voice rises sharply in excitement. 'That must be it! A glass of water.'

TWILIGHT ZONE 10

The lion is very close now.

Simmy is frozen.

'Simmy, move back! Simmy, move back!' Sammy yells.

Simmy does not move.

'Simmy!'

The lion is so close now that they can feel its hot, fetid breath. The smell is so strong that Sammy knows she's going to throw up.

She leaps up, pushes her brother out of the way and throws herself in front of the lion . . .

IN THE LIVING ROOM 4

The console beeped twice. The shape of the door lit up. Manohar shouts out loudly. 'That's it, ma'am! Glass-of-water. That's the password.'

Everyone turns towards the wall . . . it is bathed in neon light. Green and orange streaks flash across it, intensifying and moving so fast that their eyes are dazzled. All of them blink and squint, trying to keep their eyes on the wall.

The portal is opening, the corridor is visible now. Bobby dashes into the corridor.

TWILIGHT ZONE 11

The lion is licking her.

Sammy's eyes are shut tight but she can feel the rough, wet swipes on her face. *I must be losing consciousness*, she thinks.

She hears Simmy say, loudly but gently, 'Bobby, it's you, isn't it?'

Sammy hears a yelp and a bark and the sound of panting. She wills herself to open her eyes.

They are lying on the ground, and Bobby is on top of them, wagging her tail.

For some long moments, they lie there with Bobby licking their faces, just happy to be safe.

Then Simmy rolls over and hugs Sammy. 'You jumped in front of the . . . the lion or whatever it was for me. I will never forget that. I don't know if that is what saved us—but I will never forget what you did!'

Afterwards

They are in the real world, back in their bedroom.

There were hugs and kisses after they got back. Kamila had reproved their mother for bringing the work home, but Ma was too happy to care. Everyone was relieved and excited and talking at the same time.

Manohar had run a system diagnostic to confirm that there was no lingering code, no rogue AI. The game had officially been terminated. For his own satisfaction, Papa had gone around the house, checking that everything was exactly how it should be. Rejecting offers of dinner, Kamila, Aayan and Manohar had left—Kamila taking the console with her to drop off at office. 'For extra safety,' she had said sternly.

She had also told the kids a million times how brave and smart they were. Bobby's tail was a blur of happiness every time she was praised and petted for dashing into the corridor at the right moment.

And now Simmy and Sammy are in bed, after an enormous Chinese meal Ma had ordered. They are sleepy but still a little wired.

'I am so sorry,' says Ma for the hundredth time, running her hand over Simmy's head as he lies in bed.

'It's okay, Ma,' says Simmy cheerfully. 'It was fun, really.'

'Oh please,' says Sammy. Simmy is too kind. She looks at Ma reprovingly. 'Let's not get carried away now.'

'Do we have to go to school tomorrow?' Simmy asks. 'I can't do homework—my mind is a mess.'

'No, you can stay home,' Ma says. She's usually strict about school, but the kids had gone through too much. They deserved to rest and recover properly.

Bobby lifts her head from Simmy's feet and says, 'Woof.'

Papa turns off the lights while Ma tucks a duvet around Sammy.

Ma is terribly proud of the kids. They had acted with grit and determination when put through multiple scary situations—unknowingly trapped inside a game that was still not ready for the world to play. She knows that her husband is right when he says the work they do at the centre can be dangerous.

'I'm really sorry. I will make sure something like this never happens again,' Ma says softly. But Sammy and Simmy are both already fast asleep.

Ma and Papa shut the door softly behind them and walk down the corridor to their room.

They do not notice that, as the door clicks shut, a flash of green zigzag light pulses across the room.

Himanjali Sankar has written many books for children and some for adults too. Her children's and YA titles include *The Stupendous Time-telling Superdog* and *Talking of Muskaan*, both of which were shortlisted for the Crossword Book Award. Himanjali likes to use blue nail polish since it teleports her to the ocean, if she stares at her nails hard enough.

Chetan Sharma is an animator, filmmaker, writer, designer, voice actor, illustrator and singer. He started doing animation at the age of fifteen and went on to found his own animation studio, Animagic India, in 1997. He received the National Award for Best Animation in 2005 for *Raju & I,* a film on child rights. His work spans two animated feature films, six short films, a truckload of commercials, over two dozen children's books—and, of course, adoring his lovely doggie pals.